On Sunday I Lost My Cat

by *Jan Demers*

illustrated by Estella Hickman

ON SUNDAY I LOST MY CAT is one of a series of Predictable Read Together Books edited by Dr. Margaret Holland. Books in this series are designed to help young children begin to read naturally and easily. See back cover for additional information.

Published by Willowisp Press, Inc., 401 E. Wilson Bridge Road, Worthington, Ohio 43085

Library of Congress Catalog Card Number: 86-40235   ISBN 0-87406-130-X

On Monday I lost my lunch money.

On Tuesday I lost my pen.

On Wednesday I lost my homework,

so I had to do it again.

On Thursday I lost my mittens.

On Friday I lost my hat.

On Saturday I lost my sneaker.

On Sunday I lost my cat.

I looked for my cat in the cellar.

I called for her down the street.

"Have you seen my cat?" I asked everyone.

"She's black with four white feet."

On Monday I found my lunch money.

On Tuesday I found my pen.

On Wednesday I found my sneaker . . .

under the chair in the den.

On Thursday I found my hat.

On Friday I found my mittens.

On Saturday I found my cat.

And with her were two baby kittens.

On Sunday I woke up early
and jumped out of bed with a bound.

I'd thought of names for the kittens.

I called them Lost and Found.